W9-DBS-450

The Miller, the Boy and the Donkey

BASED ON A FABLE BY LA FONTAINE

The Miller, the Boy

FRANKLIN WATTS, INC.,
575 LEXINGTON AVENUE, NEW YORK, N.Y. 10022
© Brian Wildsmith 1969

First American publication 1969 by Franklin Watts, Inc.
First published 1969 by Oxford University Press
Library of Congress Catalog Card Number: 69–16607

Printed in Austria

and the Donkey

Brian Wildsmith

One morning the miller decided to take his donkey
to market and sell him.

WORTHINGTON ANDOVER LIBRARY
79-103062

So he and his boy
went out into the
field to catch him.

They took with them some carrots which the donkey loved to eat. Sure enough, when he saw the carrots the donkey came trotting towards them.

When he had eaten the carrots they took him back
to the mill and brushed his coat and polished his
hooves and combed his mane. He looked so smart
and clean the miller decided to carry him to market
to save him from dirtying his feet on the way.

They had not gone very far before they met a farmer.

He burst out laughing when he saw them. "How silly you are," he cried. "Fancy carrying a donkey! Why *he* should be carrying *you*, not *you* carrying *him*."

The miller did not like to be laughed at,

so he made the donkey start walking.

Then the boy began to feel tired and the miller lifted him on to the donkey's back.

A little further on they met three merchants who were angry when they saw the boy riding while the miller walked.

"Why, you lazy lad," they said. "Get down from the donkey and let the old man ride."

The miller made the boy get down and he

himself climbed on to the donkey's back. But it was very hot and the boy soon became tired again.

After a while they met three girls. "Shame on you, master," they called out. "How can you ride at ease while your poor boy limps so wearily behind?"

So the miller told the boy to climb up behind him, and they both rode on the donkey.

Before long they saw a priest standing outside his church. He rebuked the miller sternly. "It is cruel for both of you to ride on the back of this little animal. Have you no pity for such a faithful beast?"

With a sigh the miller climbed down and lifted the boy off the donkey. Wearily they plodded along in the hot sun, with the donkey trotting gaily beside them.

At last they came to the market-place. All the
people were amused to see the miller and his
boy trudging along in the heat of the sun, when
they might have ridden on their donkey. "The
miller is crazy," they said.

The miller sold his donkey quite quickly to a kind farmer. But his head ached from thinking about his difficult journey and all the different kinds of advice he had received. "From now on," he confided to his boy, "I shall make up my own mind, then stick to it."

The boy thought this would be an excellent idea. He nodded his head, and yawned, and they went in search of their dinner.